TEDD ARNOLD

HUGGLY'S® SNOW DAY

Cartwheel
B·O·O·K·S®

SCHOLASTIC INC.

New York   Toronto   London   Auckland   Sydney
Mexico City   New Delhi   Hong Kong   Buenos Aires

For Genevieve Young and her family—
and memories of those long-ago snow days
— T. A.

Copyright © 2002 by Tedd Arnold.
All rights reserved. Published by Scholastic Inc.
HUGGLY and THE MONSTER UNDER THE BED are trademarks and/or registered trademarks of Tedd Arnold.
SCHOLASTIC, CARTWHEEL BOOKS, and associated logos are trademarks and/or registered trademarks of Scholastic Inc.

Library of Congress Cataloging-in-Publication Data available.

ISBN 0-439-32447-5

12 11 10 9 8 7 6 5 4 3   02 03 04 05 06

Printed in the U.S.A.
First printing, January 2002

Huggly hurried into the Secret Slime Pit. "Hey, Booter! Grubble! Come quick!" he cried. "Something is wrong with the people world!"

"What is it?" asked Booter.

"It's GONE!" said Huggly. "The people world is gone!"

"This is not a good time for jokes," said Grubble. "We're busy trying to figure out why the slime pit is as hard as a rock."

"Maybe it's hard because it's so cold in here," said Booter. "Good thing us monsters don't mind the cold."

"I'm not joking!" insisted Huggly. "The people world is gone. Come see for yourselves."

Huggly led Booter and Grubble to the hatchway under his favorite people bed.

"Wait a minute," said Grubble. "Before I go up there, tell me exactly what's missing. Is the people house gone?"

"No, the house is fine," said Huggly.
"So what's the problem?" asked Grubble.
"*Shhh*!" Huggly whispered. "Don't wake the people child on the bed. We don't want to get caught!"

They tiptoed across the room to the window. "*There* is the problem," said Huggly. "The people world outside is gone!"

Looking through the window, all they could see was white.

"I need a closer look," Booter whispered. "How can we get outside?"

"Follow me," said Huggly.

Huggly led them downstairs to a doorway that was cluttered with people things.

"This is the way out," he said.

He pulled the door open, and
ran—*WHUMP!*—right into a wall
of white stuff.

"What is *this*?" asked Huggly.

"I don't know," said Booter.

"Not much flavor," said Grubble.

"Hey! I can see the sky outside," said Huggly. He scrambled over the pile of white powder. Booter and Grubble followed.

"Yippee!" cried Huggly. "The people world is still here. It's just covered up with all this stuff."

He scooped up a handful and began patting and shaping it.
"Look, I can make this into a ba . . ." *WHAP!* Something
smacked him on the back.

"Into a *ball*?" asked Grubble, laughing. "Is that what you
were going to say?" Then—*WHAP!*—something hit Grubble.

"Yeah," said Booter. "That's what he was going to say."

Suddenly, Huggly, Booter, and Grubble were all making white balls as fast as they could. They chased each other around the backyard, throwing and ducking and laughing. After a while, they collapsed into the white stuff, out of breath and giggling.

After a moment, Booter stood back up. "Look what I made!" she said.

"And look at this," said Huggly. "The white stuff is great for making things!"

Quickly they went to
work making bigger and
bigger shapes.

"Uh-oh! The sky is starting to get light," said Booter.

"The people will be waking up soon," said Huggly. "We need to get back under the bed."

They looked around at the white stuff and felt sad that they had to leave.

"Why don't we take some back with us?" said Huggly.

"But monsters aren't supposed to take people things," Booter reminded them.

Huggly looked up. "This stuff is falling from the sky," he said. "I think it's free for everybody. Even monsters."

"I agree," said Grubble.

"Okay," said Booter. "We'd better hurry."

They rolled up a ball so big that
it took all three of them to carry it.

Through the house, up the stairs,
and into the bedroom they ran.

Carefully, without a
sound, they pushed
the ball under the bed.

Once in the monster world, thay raced away to the Secret Slime Pit.

"Grubble!" cried Huggly. "What did you do with all the white stuff!"

"I didn't do anything with it," said Grubble.

"Oh, yeah?" said Huggly. "Well, now there isn't enough left to have any fun!"

"You're wrong," said Grubble, and he hit Huggly with the white ball. "See? That was fun!" he said.

"No fair," Huggly complained. "I can't get you back because I don't have anything to throw!"

"Don't fight, you two," said Booter. "Let's just go get some more."

Quickly they returned to the back door. Booter and Grubble scooped up another big ball.

"Wait," said Huggly. "Maybe we won't lose so much if we carry it back in these boxes."

"Now you're thinking!" said Booter.

Working as fast as they could,

Huggly, Booter, and Grubble carried

load after load of the white stuff

down to their Secret Slime Pit.

They worked until the people mother came into the bedroom.

"Guess what, sleepyhead?" she said. "It's been snowing all night. There's no school today."

The people child leaped out of the bed. "Hurray!" he shouted. "IT'S A SNOW DAY!"

He dressed as fast as he could and raced downstairs. Pausing just long enough to pull on his coat and boots, he threw open the back door and . . .

couldn't believe his eyes!

Down in the Secret Slime Pit, the monsters were having fun.

"I wonder," said Huggly. "Just as we were closing the hatchway under the bed, I heard the people child say something about a 'snow day.' What do you think he was talking about?"

"Maybe this white stuff is called 'snow'," said Booter.

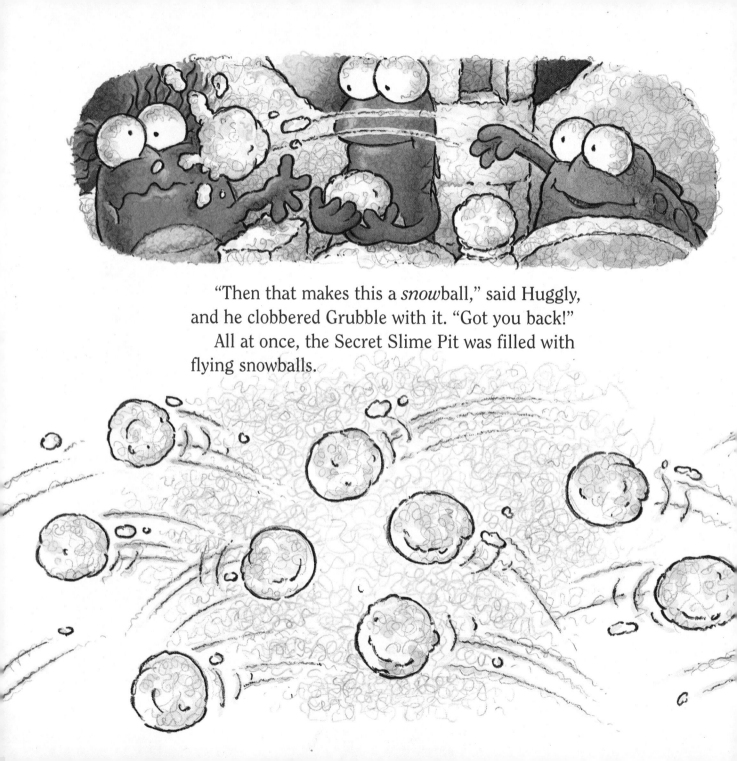

"Then that makes this a *snow*ball," said Huggly,
and he clobbered Grubble with it. "Got you back!"
All at once, the Secret Slime Pit was filled with
flying snowballs.

LOOK FOR THESE OTHER BOOKS IN THIS SERIES:

Huggly and the Toy Monster
Huggly Goes to School
Huggly's Pizza
Huggly's Christmas
Huggly's Big Mess

LAUGH ALONG WITH HUGGLY® AND THE MONSTERS UNDER THE BED?

Huggly and his friends live in the monster world. But sometimes the human world is just too hard to resist! That's when the fun begins. . . .

Huggly looks outside and thinks the "People World" has disappeared. It's not gone—just covered with SNOW! Can Huggly and his friends get some of this cool stuff back to the Secret Slime Pit before it melts? Find out when you join Huggly in this laugh-out-loud adventure!

Lovable Huggly and his friends are monsters every child will want to meet!

ISBN 0-439-32447-5

50325

EAN

9 780439 324472

$3.25 US
$4.25 CAN

Cartwheel
B·O·O·K·S®

SCHOLASTIC INC.